Robin Overcomes

By

Bryant Johnson

Illustrated by
Kids_art

This book is dedicated to my two daughters Kaylen and Skylar. You be everything God has called you to be. There is no one who can be a better you than YOU.

Robin the robin was the nicest bird in town.
Robin was so nice the other birds would all surround,
and although Robin was the nicest bird in town,
Robin never did like when Eldridge came around.

Now Eldridge the eagle was quite profound,
Eldridge would say, "I'm smart and I'm crowned
the most celebrated bird that's ever been found."
Eldridge would crow so much his head became round.

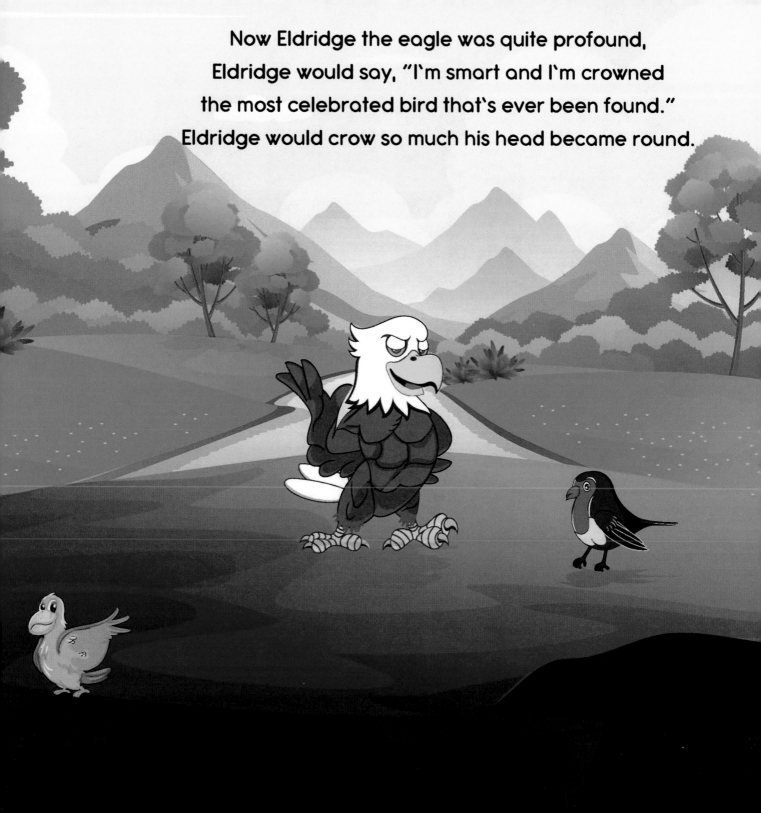

"My feathers are the most beautiful color brown.
And I can fly so high that my wings touch the clouds!"
And even though Eldridge was the biggest and proud,
Robin would still frown when that eagle came around.

Eldridge would eat all the food and snatch all the berries
and would even take the fish from Gary and Gerry.

Eldridge would go out to Pierre and plunder in the prairie.
He was known to get aggressive and attack.
That's when he'd spread his wings and get real scary,
when Mary the meerkat would go to get the food scraps back.

KEE-KEE!!
KEE-KEE!!

One day Eldridge was up to no good rummaging in a mound, when a piece of plastic wrapped around his neck and pinned him to the ground.
Eldridge grew frantic, he squawked and squealed real loud.
The other animals noticed, but none of them came inbound.

A far-off Robin heard a noise.
This noise had Robin astounded.
But Robin was even more astounded
the other animals had not surrounded.

The others knew Eldridge wasn't friendly,
so helping him was out of the discussion,
but Robin had too kind of a heart
to just sit around and do nothing.

That's when Robin swooped
down toward the sound
to help Eldridge with that plastic
that had his head bound.

"I`M FREE!! I`M FREE!!" Eldridge cried aloud.

He walked up to Robin and got real close......

"THANK YOU!! THANK YOU!!" he shouted.

"Robin is the greatest friend I have ever had,
and my days of being a rude fowl are over,
might I add!"

That day, Robin was crowned the nicest and bravest bird in town, and Robin and Eldridge hung out any time he was around.

About the Author

Bryant Johnson is a newly published author. Exhausted from buying daughters books at the store, he thought it would save time and money to make stories for them. Creating stories would soon turn into a passion and a way to inspire through creativity. He is a God fearing husband to Symphonie and father of two living in San Diego. With a creative mind and countless ideas and thought provoking images to share with the world, what better time than now to let his voice be heard.

Have not I commanded thee? Be strong and of a good courage; be not afraid, neither be thou dismayed: for the LORD thy God is with thee whithersoever thou goest.

Joshua 1:9

The Student Bible, King James Version.
Zondervan Publishing House,
1992, 1996

Made in the USA
Middletown, DE
15 June 2021